Waiting for
Christmas

A Story about the Advent Calendar

Written by Kathleen Long Bostrom
Illustrated by Alexi Natchev

zonderkidz

zonderkidz
The children's group
of Zondervan

www.zonderkidz.com

Waiting for Christmas
Copyright © 2006 by Kathleen Long Bostrom • Illustrations © 2006 by Alexi Natchev
Requests for information should be addressed to: Grand Rapids, Michigan 49530

CIP Applied for

ISBN-10: 0-310-71015-4 • ISBN-13: 978-0-310-71015-8

Editor: Amy De Vries • Art direction and design: Laura Maitner-Mason

Printed in China

06 07 08 09 10 • 10 9 8 7 6 5 4 3 2 1

In honor of Jan and Don Wolverton, and Dottie and Marshal Hill:

You helped me find my way in life, and I will always be grateful. — K.L.B.

Yet the LORD longs to be gracious to you;
he rises to show you compassion.
For the LORD is a God of justice.
Blessed are all who wait for him!
(Isaiah 30:18)

Author's Note

Advent is the season before Christmas in which we prepare for the birth of Jesus Christ and for his coming again into the world. The celebration of Advent began as early as the fourth century. The word *Advent* comes from the Latin *ad,* which means "toward," and *vent*, which means "come."

Christians living in Germany often marked their doors with twenty-four lines at the beginning of Advent, and erased one line each day until Christmas. Some families hung twenty-four little pictures on their walls, while others placed one piece of straw in a manger each day for twenty-four days.

It wasn't until 1851 that the first Advent calendars came into being. Gerhard Lang, the son of a Protestant minister and his wife, is credited with making the Advent calendar available to the public. Gerhard had fond memories of the Advent calendars his mother made for him when he was young. She tied small *Wibele,* or traditional German cookies, onto a sheet of cardboard—one cookie for each day of Advent.

When Gerhard became a partner in the Reichhold & Lang printing company, he began publishing miniature colored pictures on a sheet of cardboard. This first printed Advent calendar was published in 1908.

The Advent calendar spread throughout the world. During World War II, however, cardboard was rationed, and Advent calendars were not made commercially. Since then many varieties of Advent calendars have come into being, including calendars filled with chocolates.

This delightful worldwide tradition evolved from the creativity of a German mother seeking a way to help her young son count down the days until Christmas.

"Mama, how many days 'til Christmas?" Gerhard asked.

"As soon as it is December, we'll start to count down the days. Good things are worth waiting for, Gerhard," replied Mama.

"But it is hard to wait," Gerhard complained.

"I know," his mother said, "but if you keep busy, the time will pass more quickly. Now run and take this bread and cheese to your papa."

Gerhard's father was the pastor of their church. He was starting to work longer hours to get everything ready for Christmas. Gerhard hurried across the town square with his father's supper.

A shop window filled with amazing Christmas treats caught his eye. He had never seen such a fantastic display. Cakes, cookies, and candies of all shapes and sizes were laid out around a small Christmas tree.

He ran on and burst through the front door of the church.

"Papa! Papa! Have you seen the shop full of Christmas sweets! I *can't wait* to see what special treats Oma and Opa will bring me this year."

"Even baby Jesus had to wait for his first Christmas gifts," Papa said.

Gerhard suddenly stood still. "Really?" he asked.

Papa smiled. "Oh, yes. Two or three years after Jesus was born, the wise men brought their gifts to him."

"He waited two or three *years*?" Gerhard's eyes opened wide. "I could never wait *that* long!"

"Advent begins this Sunday," he said. "Then you may start counting down the days until Christmas. Until then, we have much to do to prepare for Jesus' birth. Mama and I need your help if we are to be ready."

When Gerhard returned home, Mama was making Lebkuchen, a special Christmas cookie. He helped measure the sugared fruits and added them to the dough. The colorful fruits made him think about the special treats his grandparents would be bringing for Christmas.

"We have to let the dough set overnight before we can bake these," said his mother.

"I have to wait for cookies too?" Gerhard asked.

Mama kissed the top of Gerhard's head. "It takes a long time to make Lebkuchen before it is ready to be eaten."

The next day the dough was ready to be baked into delicious cookies.

"Gerhard, I think Papa needs help decorating the church today."

"But Mama, I want to help you bake cookies!" said Gerhard.

Mama smiled, a twinkle in her eye. "Not today, my little son. Today, you need to help your papa."

Gerhard brought in pine branches to decorate the windows and pews of the church. He helped tie them together. The pine smelled wonderful. Then he placed the tall white candles in the windows and on the altar. These would be lit on Christmas Eve. Though his hands were busy, Gerhard couldn't stop thinking about all the fun he would have on Christmas Day.

Later that afternoon when Gerhard returned home, the whole house smelled of delicious spices and honey. "Mama, may I have a cookie now? They smell so good!"

"Not yet," Mama replied. "The cookies must be placed in a tin box and left for a few weeks before they will be ready to eat."

"Weeks!" cried Gerhard.

"For now, you can draw the chalk lines on our door," she said. "That will help you count the days of Advent."

"Draw twenty-four lines. Starting tomorrow, you may erase one line each night before you go to bed. When all the lines are gone, it will be Christmas Eve."

"Twenty-four days. That's a long time," Gerhard said.

Gerhard wondered if Christmas would *ever* arrive.

The first day of Advent finally arrived. "Gerhard, I have a surprise for you that may make it easier to wait for Christmas," said Mama.

"What is it, Mama? Please tell me!"

She pointed to the dining room table. Something was underneath the tablecloth. Gerhard lifted a corner and peeked underneath.

"Oh, Mama!" he squealed in delight. "*Wibele!* My favorite cookie!"

"There is one cookie for every day of December until Christmas," she explained. "After supper, you may have one cookie, every evening until Christmas Eve. This should make the waiting sweeter."

"Thank you, Mama!" Gerhard gave her a big hug.

That night, Gerhard erased the first chalk line from the door. He untied his first Advent cookie and shared it with Mama and Papa.

"Was it hard for Mary and Joseph to wait for Jesus to be born?" he asked Papa.

"Yes," he answered. "But Mary and Joseph weren't the only ones. The whole world had waited thousands of years for Jesus to come. When the time finally came, the angels in heaven and the earth sang songs of joy. Someday Jesus will come again."

"A thousand years!" Gerhard exclaimed. I couldn't fit that many cookies on a calendar."

Papa laughed. "You would need a *very* large calendar for that many cookies!"

Before going to bed, Gerhard closed his eyes and prayed,
"Thank you, dear God, for Mama and Papa and Oma and
Opa and for candies and treats and Christmas. But thank you
most of all for Jesus. And God, help me to be patient. Amen."

Gerhard snuggled down into his blankets. Christmas would
come, he knew. For now, he would just have to wait. But that
was all right.

Some things were
worth waiting for.

Keeping the Tradition

Advent Chain #1

Cut twenty-four strips of paper, one inch wide and five or six inches long. Tape, glue, or staple one strip into a circle. Make each circle connect through the previous circle. When you are finished, you will have an Advent chain to hang on a Christmas tree or in some other prominent place in your home. Remove one circle on the chain, starting on the first day of Advent, and continue to remove one more each day. When the chain is gone, it will be Christmas Eve!

Advent Chain #2

As with the first chain, cut twenty-four strips of paper. Write an activity on each strip. For example: "Pray for someone who is sick," "Take cookies to a neighbor," "Call a relative on the phone," "Sing Christmas or Advent carols." Everyone in the family might have a special day on which that person gets to pick the dinner menu or a movie to watch. On each day during Advent, a person chooses a strip of paper from the basket and decides when to perform the activity. As you prepare for the birth of Jesus, you are giving "gifts" to others in the acts of kindness that you do.

The Art Wall

Before the Advent calendar, children drew pictures and hung them on the wall. Set aside twenty-four pieces of paper, and each day draw a picture to hang. After Christmas, you can collect the pictures in an album or send them to friends and relatives.

Cut-and-Paste Pictures

Take a sheet of paper or cardboard and divide it into twenty-four squares. On each square write a number from one to twenty-four. Each day during Advent, find a pretty picture in a magazine in the right size to cover the square. Cut and paste the pictures onto the squares, starting with #1 and continuing through #24. Now you have your own Advent calendar.

Treat Calendar

Make your own Advent calendar like Gerhard's first one! Tie twenty-four pieces of candy or cookies onto a piece of cardboard you have decorated for Christmas. Remove one treat each day (be sure everyone in the family gets a turn!).